Dear Parent:

Congratulations! Your child is taking the first steps on an exciting journey. The destination? Independent reading!

STEP INTO READING® will help your child get there. The program offers five steps to reading success. Each step includes fun stories and colorful art. There are also Step into Reading Sticker Books, Step into Reading Math Readers, Step into Reading Phonics Readers, Step into Reading Write-In Readers, and Step into Reading Phonics Boxed Sets—a complete literacy program with something to interest every child.

Learning to Read, Step by Step!

Ready to Read   Preschool–Kindergarten
• big type and easy words • rhyme and rhythm • picture clues
For children who know the alphabet and are eager to begin reading.

Reading with Help   Preschool–Grade 1
• basic vocabulary • short sentences • simple stories
For children who recognize familiar words and sound out new words with help.

Reading on Your Own   Grades 1–3
• engaging characters • easy-to-follow plots • popular topics
For children who are ready to read on their own.

Reading Paragraphs   Grades 2–3
• challenging vocabulary • short paragraphs • exciting stories
For newly independent readers who read simple sentences with confidence.

Ready for Chapters   Grades 2–4
• chapters • longer paragraphs • full-color art
For children who want to take the plunge into chapter books but still like colorful pictures.

STEP INTO READING® is designed to give every child a successful reading experience. The grade levels are only guides. Children can progress through the steps at their own speed, developing confidence in their reading, no matter what their grade.

Remember, a lifetime love of reading starts with a single step!

Visit us on the Web!
StepIntoReading.com
randomhouse.com/kids

Educators and librarians, for a variety of teaching tools, visit us at RHTeachersLibrarians.com

ISBN: 978-0-7364-2886-6 (trade) — ISBN: 978-0-7364-8113-7 (lib. bdg.)

Printed in the United States of America   10 9 8 7 6 5 4 3 2 1

DISNEY · PIXAR
Cars

Mater
and the
Little Tractors

Adapted by Chelsea Eberly

Illustrated by Andy Phillipson,
Scott Tilley, David Boelke and
the Disney Storybook Artists

Random House 🏠 New York

One morning,
Mater was making
a music box.

It was a surprise
for his friends.

The music box
was done!
Mater hooked it
to his towline.
He headed
to Main Street.

Mater showed
the music box
to Ramone.
Ramone was
too busy to look.

A little tractor
was painting
his shop!

Mater showed
the music box
to Lightning McQueen.
Lightning was busy.
He was chasing
a runaway tractor.

Mater took

the music box

to Luigi's tire shop.

Luigi was busy,
too.
A little tractor
had knocked over
a tower of tires!

Mater took
the music box
to Red.

Red was crying.
Little tractors
had crushed
his flowers!

Mater took
the music box
to Sheriff.

Sheriff could not
look at it.
He had
to catch
the little tractors!

The little tractors
were everywhere!
One was using
Ramone's paint.

One was playing
with Red's flowers.

One was eating
Luigi's tires.

The little tractors
were making a mess!

Mater's friends
needed his help.
He had an idea.

Mater turned on
his music box.
A shy little tractor
followed him.

Mater drove slowly
down the street.
More little tractors
followed him.

Mater looked back.
The little tractors
loved the music!
He made it louder.

25

The little tractors

followed the music

into the junkyard.

The fence would

keep them inside.

Everyone cheered!

The tractors could not
cause any more trouble.
Sheriff thanked Mater.

The little tractors
danced in circles.
Mater and his friends
watched.
They all had fun.

Mater's music box

had saved the day!